W9-AGU-660

A Gift For:

....

From:

....

Copyright © 2014 Hallmark Licensing, LLC

Published by Hallmark Gift Books,
a division of Hallmark Cards, Inc.,
Kansas City, MO 64141
Visit us on the Web at Hallmark.com.

All rights reserved. No part of this publication may be
reproduced, transmitted, or stored in any form or by any
means without the prior written permission of the publisher.

Editorial Director: Delia Berrigan
Editor: Nate Barbarick
Art Director: Jan Mastin
Designer: Mark Voss
Writer: Diana Manning
Illustrator: Matt Kesler
Production Designer: Dan Horton

ISBN: 978-1-59530-864-1
MJJ1012

Printed and bound in China
JUN14

If you have enjoyed this book
or it has touched your life in some way,
we would love to hear from you.

Please send your comments to:
Hallmark Book Feedback
P.O. Box 419034
Mail Drop 100
Kansas City, MO 64141

Or e-mail us at:
booknotes@hallmark.com

NORTHPOLE
EST. 1820

ONCE UPON A NORTHPOLE
CHRISTMAS

By Noel Manning · Illustrated by Sledd Kesler

Hallmark

Have you ever heard
the incredible story
of happiness, magic, and snow?
How a wee little elf
made a wondrous discovery
one Christmas not so long ago?

The elves had all gathered
  outside in the square—
    they'd noticed that something was wrong.
It soon would be Christmas,
  and every elf knew
    that snow should be coming down strong.

"What was the matter?"
  they started to wonder
    with snow barely falling at all—
They knew this could turn out
  to be a disaster—
    the worst they could ever recall!

Because snow is the magic
  that powers Northpole—
    each delicate flake gets its start
as a sparkle that forms
  and invisibly rises
    from happiness felt in the heart.

Then each spark of happiness
  rises up high
    to put on a beautiful show…
They shimmer and shine
  as the great Northern Lights
    before they start falling as snow.

"There must not have been
    enough happiness shared!"
        the elves and their families cried.
"How will we get
    enough toy-making magic
        to keep our great city supplied?"

Santa assured them
    they'd all done their part
        to handle the Christmas Eve crunch—
their beacons would help him
    get toys to the children,
        and cookies left out would be munched!

"Every little bit counts,"
he reminded them all
as he patted a little elf's head.
"Even the smallest
of snowflakes can roll
into one giant snowball," he said.

The wee little elf
scurried off to the forest
as quiet and quick as could be—
He hurried to check on
the glimmering globes
that hung from each glistening tree.

Each globe is a magical window,
  of sorts,
    for those of us here in Northpole
  to see all the families
    preparing for Christmas—
      a wonderful sight to behold!

Without any happiness
  fueling the magic
    for what Northpole's all about,
Our work here would come
  to a stop, I'm afraid . . .
    just imagine how things could turn out!

Without it, there wouldn't be
    cozy elf cottages
        glowing with twinkling lights—
no high-flying reindeer
    to pull Santa's sleigh
        on his round-the-world Christmas Eve flight.

There wouldn't be cocoa
   or Mrs. Claus's cookies
      with sprinkles as sweet as could be—
and worst of all,
      there'd be no toys from the toy guilds
      for kids to find under the tree.

The little elf noticed
   the globes which were dimming
      showed people with no time to share—
trying too hard
   to make Christmas too perfect
      or running around everywhere.

They were off on their own
looking grumpy and tired,
with hardly a smile to be found—
too busy for carols
and moments of merry
with loved ones and family around.

All of a sudden,
  the wee little elf
    had a lightbulb light up in his head—
He gathered his friends
    for a special assignment—
      "I've got an idea!" he said.

The elf kids wrote millions
and zillions of notes,
not stopping until they were done—
The notes all flew down
in a magical swirl
with the name of a child on each one.

Soon it was time
   to look in on the globes,
      as the Christmas Eve Watch Party started.
With hardly a flurry
   or flake to be seen,
      the folks were all feeling downhearted—

Except for the elf kids,
   who whispered and giggled
      while anxiously milling about—
They were quietly hoping
   their plan had succeeded
      and just couldn't wait to find out!

Just then, the wee elf
    tugged on Santa's red coat—
        "Sir, I think there's a globe you should see . . ."
He pointed them all
    to the half-hidden glow
        on the bottommost branch of a tree.

They bent down to look
   at the heartwarming scene—
      the elf said "A family's the cause!"
"They're reading a story,
   and look—they're so happy!"
      which started a round of applause.

They noticed another globe
  coming to life
    with the laughter a family was sharing.
Then another one here . . .
    and another one there . . .
      every elf was excitedly staring!

The wee little elf
  knew it wasn't just toys
    that brought happiness this time of year.
"True happiness comes
    from what families share
      as they gather when Christmas is near"

All over the world
    people started to see
        how they'd missed what the season is for.
So they gathered with loved ones
    in homes far and wide,
        making memories together once more.

The children had all
    brought their loved ones together—
        those zillions of notes did the trick.
Soon snow started falling…
    and falling… and falling…
        all fluffy and puffy and thick!

Carefully taking
  one globe in her hand,
    with the wee little elf by her side,
  Mrs. Santa Claus carried it
    all through the forest,
      showing the others with pride.

"Here is the globe
  that burns brightest," she said,
    as she held it, as light as a feather.
"It glows with the happiness
  families share
    as long as they spend time together."

"What did I tell you?
    We're back up and running!"
        said Santa Claus, bending down low.
"Even the smallest
    of snowflakes can roll
        into one giant snowball, you know!"

Everyone cheered
  as they heard the good news . . .
    I was there and I saw it myself!
Although it's been years,
  I remember it well . . .
    because I was that wee little elf!

And Christmas this year?
　　Well the answer's the same
　　　　as it was in that long-ago note—
It's something that everyone
　　needs to remember,
　　　　so here is the message we wrote:

Dear little friend
  south of Northpole,

We're hoping this finds you. . . and fast!
  Without help from you,
  Christmas, it seems,
might become just a thing of the past!

  We need more happiness
    to make the magic
that's powered Northpole from the start!
  How can you help?
  You don't have to look far—
the answer is right in your heart.

  Spread holiday cheer,
    give hugs to your family—
there's really so much you can do!
  The more love you share,
the more magic you'll make—
  the elves are all counting on you!